September 2018

For
Lucas and
Adelyn

Love Nana

Library of Congress Cataloging-in-Publication
Data Available

ISBN 978-0-545-86501-2

10 9 8 7 6 5 4 3 2 1   17 18 19 20 21

Printed in Malaysia 108
First edition, April 2017
The text type and display type are
hand lettered by Peter H. Reynolds.

Reynolds Studio assistance by Julia Anne Young

Book design by Patti Ann Harris

HAPPY
DREAMER
by PETER H. REYNOLDS

ORCHARD BOOKS

AN IMPRINT of SCHOLASTIC INC.
NEW YORK

I AM A HAPPY DREAMER.

I'm really good at dreaming.

DAY DREAMS.

BIG DREAMS.

Little dreams.

CREATIVE DREAMS.

DIZZY HAPPY

ART HAPPY

MOVE HAPPY

DREAMY DREAMER

TEAM DREAMER

VISION DREAMER

HARD WORK HAPPY

CELEBRATION HAPPY

LAUGH HAPPY

GOAL DREAMER

STAGE DREAMER

STELLAR DREAMER

NATURE HAPPY

DISCOVERY HAPPY

FAMILY HAPPY

NIGHT DREAMER

DAYDREAMER

BIG DREAMER

ALONE HAPPY

FRIENDS HAPPY

OCEAN HAPPY

SPACE DREAMER

FIERCE DREAMER

GIANT DREAMER

THERE ARE SO MANY WAYS TO BE A
HAPPY DREAMER!

(WHAT KIND OF DREAMER ARE YOU?)

But the best way
to be a happy dreamer?

I have so many dreams it can get messy.
CREATIVE CHAOS.

Cleaning up hides my treasures.

IF YOU MAKE ME,
I will put my things away.
But then there is
less ME to show.

These are the moments
I feel alone.

BOXED IN.

And yet, I always find a way back.

Plunging into amazing, delightful, happy dreams.

I'm really good
at being me.

A DREAMER

SURPRISING

CARING

FUNNY

GENTLE

SMART

And when I
TUMBLE
back to earth...

I Know I'm Okay!

Dreamers have a way of bouncing back...

AND MOVING FORWARD!

WINGED DREAMER

ROYAL DREAMER

THINKING DREAMER

SWEET DREAMER

SUNNY DREAMER

FLOATING DREAMER

LOVE DREAMER

WILD DREAMER

CRAZY DREAMER

POWER DREAMER

CIVIC DREAMER

SECRET DREAMER

ICE CREAM HAPPY

SUNSHINE HAPPY

MAKE A DIFFERENCE HAPPY

NAP HAPPY

MUSIC HAPPY

DANCE HAPPY

PEACEFUL HAPPY

CATCH HAPPY

KINDNESS HAPPY

AWE HAPPY

SILLY HAPPY

FOOT-STOMPIN' HAPPY

dreamer maximus!

Sometimes the world tells me ...

SIT STILL.

BE QUIET.

But my dreams have
a mind of their own.

SOMETIMES MY MIND JUST TAKES FLIGHT! I HEAR A **BEAT** AND I GOTTA MOVE...

THEN I HEAR ANOTHER AND ANOTHER!

TRUMPETY, ZIGZAG JAZZ!

Sometimes I'm a
quiet dreamer

when I make time
to stay still and
hear myself think—
to let go and see
what takes shape.

DO YOU SEE THAT?

Sometimes I'm a swing-high dreamer... WAY UP HIGH...BEYOND THE CLOUDS...

SO HIGH I CAN TOUCH THE SKY!

I can also be a **LOUD** dreamer!

HELLO,

WORLD!

I'M A SHOUT-AT-THE-TOP-OF-MY-LUNGS DREAMER!

(EVEN IF I'M JUST A LOUD-INSIDE-MY-HEAD DREAMER!)

SOMETIMES...

I'M A COLORFUL DREAMER,

PAINTING MY OWN PATH
FULL OF SURPRISES AT EVERY TURN.

I can dream
even when the
lights are OUT.

ALL CIRCUITS ON!
FIREWORKS!
I LIGHT UP!
I'M ALL EARS,
EYES, HEART, AND MIND!

Just **BE** YOU.

Which is why this book is dedicated to you. YES, YOU!